A Rhino to the

A Tale of Conservation and Adventure

Written and Illustrated By
Cleve Hicks

In Cleve Hicks' book, A Rhino to the Rescue, *children can be made aware of the struggles and near extinction of our beautiful wild rhinos. Through his whimsical paintings and story, the reader can gain insight in this very important conservation effort. The truth is sometimes brutal and Cleve did a great job of getting the main point across. We all need to be better caretakers of our planet!*

—Author, Doreen Ingram
www.myplacecalledhome.com

SUSANNA LAGOON™ Books
An imprint of J. K. Eckert and Company, Inc.
Nokomis, FL 34275
www.jkeckert.com

ISBN: 978-0-9913571-9-2

Interior design by J.K. Eckert & Company, Inc.

Illustrations and text by Cleve Hicks

DEDICATIONS

Gaurab Sarangi—*Mere paas hai tu, mere paas hai, mere saath hai. Nahin Saamne, A. R. Rahman.*

My parents, Thurston and Kitty Hicks—When I was a kid, my dad would bring me books from the Raleigh Public Library. I would listen, spellbound, as he and my mom read me countless splendid tales about animals and adventures in faraway places.

Sonia Uribe—*A mi amada compañera de viaje y compañera de vida: ¡Tenemos mucho mas por explorar juntos!*

Additional thanks to my mom Kitty Hicks and to Judy Song for all their feedback and encouragement on early drafts of the book, and to fellow author, Doreen Ingram, for working so hard to help me share Ernest's tale with the world. Thanks also to Susan Shiau for her help with the Chinese text, as well as Savannah and Isaiah Hicks, my first and kindest reviewers.

One fine day, Ernest Horningway, a large and gentle fellow
of the rhinoceros kind, was sipping a sweet and colorful
rainbow swirler while enjoying the company of his even

larger friend, a distinguished elephant named Ogoro Sartorius. The two had spent the morning munching on crumpets and discussing the news of the day.

Ernest and Sartorius had been devoted friends for many years, and they frequently visited one another's homes, which rested on some rolling hills on the outskirts of Puddington, England.

Sartorius interrupted the pleasant mood to show his friend a story in the newspaper. "You see here, dear Ernest, our wild cousins in Africa and Asia are being killed, just so people can sell their horns and tusks!"

Ernest tried to turn the conversation to a more uplifting topic—such as the price of jellybeans in Argentina—but Sartorius would not permit it. "This subject is much too important!" he trumpeted.

The terrible news drew a frown across Ernest's normally jolly face. It was painful to learn that people would slaughter such gentle creatures just to sell their horns. He leaped to his feet and declared, "I'm going to meet my wild cousins and do something to help!"

Sartorius replied with a satisfied grin, "I know just where you can find them!"

The two friends retreated into the living room and pulled out a map of Africa. "Take a look here," rumbled the old elephant, pointing toward the middle of the map with his trunk. "Rhinoceroses were once found all across the continent of Africa. Lately, I am afraid, they have largely disappeared from the wild, but you can still find them in Kenya."

"I'll buy an airplane ticket now," declared Ernest. "It's time I went and met my wild cousins!"

Although they had invited their neighbors, the Hippopoddingtons, to dinner the following night, Ernest knew they would understand the urgency of his mission, and asked Sartorius to explain to them his sudden change of plans.

After calling a taxi, Ernest gathered his umbrella, a
suitable, and a suitable collection of colorful cravats
(an old-fashioned kind of necktie) and rushed out the door.

6

Sartorius trumpeted cheerily after him, "Have a lovely trip...and don't forget to greet my elephant cousins!"

The next day, after a very long flight, Ernest arrived at a small airport in Kenya.

Tired and a little grouchy from being squeezed into a seat much too small for his size, Ernest searched for a guide to take him to meet the wild rhinoceroses.

Although most folks seemed friendly, Ernest noticed a couple of men nearby eyeing his *nose horn* with worrying interest.

At that moment, a cheerful voice called out to Ernest.

"Friend! Welcome to Kenya. My name is Seba. Hop on my boda-boda, and I'll take you to the national park to meet the wild rhinos!"

Ernest liked the look of this fellow, and hoisted himself onto the back of his bike.

Before long, the two had left the crowded town far behind. As they drove down a dusty country road, they passed gazelles, giraffes, elephants, and even a hippopoto-mom with her roly-poly baby trundling to the nearest water hole!

Finally they entered the national park. Seba smiled and drove toward some pointy-snouted shapes on the horizon. "There are your rhinos, my friend!" he proudly announced.

Seba, who had to get back to town to continue his work as a driver, left Ernest by the roadside and sped off. As he left,

he called out to his new friend, "See you in a few weeks! Best of luck and please be careful—those rhinos are not very used to townsfolk." Ernest nodded and waved goodbye.

Excited to finally meet his cousins, he pulled out a portable table, poured himself a *rainbow swirler*, and waited patiently for the wild rhinos to approach him.

The wild rhinoceroses were puzzled by this strangely dressed intruder. Although he looked just like them, his fancy clothes and umbrella seemed very out of place.

One of the members of the rhino family was a hot-headed young bull named Likambo. He did not at all like the look of

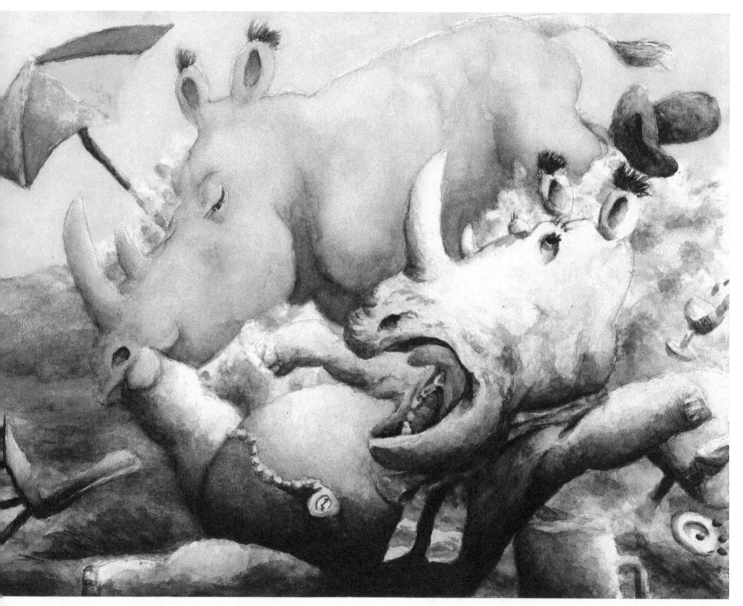

this city slicker. Likambo snorted out a warning, and then
lowered his head and charged toward Ernest, who was
happily entertaining himself by munching on an olive.

Ernest was surrounded by hostile wild rhinoceroses. He feared the worst, and indeed was terrified for his life.

Fortunately, a wise and powerful rhinoceros elder, Wilhelmina, could tell by looking at him that Ernest was a kindly soul. Pushing the others aside, she calmly accepted his presence into the clan.

Although she spoke no English, Wilhelmina communicated to Ernest through her sounds and actions. She let him know that no harm would come to him and that he was now a welcome visitor.

That night, Wilhelmina led Ernest to a lonely waterhole. What had once been a place of happy rhinoceros reunions and romances was now nothing but a gloomy graveyard. Human hunters, hidden in the bushes, had shot several rhinos as they approached to drink the fresh water. They had then used machetes to cut the horns off the rhinos' heads to sell them to foreign markets.

Ernest, struck with grief as he gazed upon the bleached white skeletons scattered around the pool, vowed to help Wilhelmina and the other rhinos. This was not a time for *rainbow swirlers*—this was serious and dangerous business!

24

Over the next month, Ernest lived with his cousins and learned the ways of the wild rhino—how to find the choicest cuts of grass, and to snort deeply and sniff the winds for signs of danger. Likambo even taught him how to charge, thunderously! The hardest lesson for the haughty Ernest to learn was how to keep his head down while charging. When he did it right, he looked and felt as fearless as Likambo.

Finally the time came for Ernest to leave his newfound
friends. The wild rhinos stood along the roadside and

watched as he sped off on the back of Seba's boda-boda, kicking up a trail of savannah dust. For the first time in years, they allowed themselves to feel some hope. "Don't you all worry!" Ernest yelled. "I have a doozy of a plan."

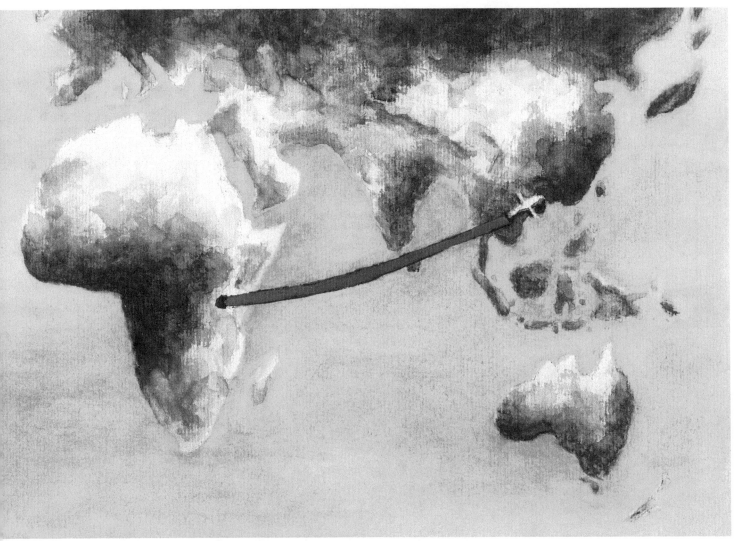

It was time to board another airplane. This time Ernest flew to a place called Hong Kong in Asia. He had learned from

Sartorius that this was where smugglers sold much of their
rhino horn and elephant ivory on the world market.

He went immediately to meet Wildlife Officer Hou Che-ying.

30

"People would pay big money for that lovely horn on your snout—they think it's medicine," explained Officer Hou (pronounced *Who*), "but it's made of the same stuff as our fingernails. Drinking rhino horn tea is as worthless as slurping down a bowl of fingernail soup!"

"This must be stopped!" Ernest was angry. "Where can we find the smugglers?"

"They often unload their merchandise at Victoria Harbor. Sadly, we don't have the evidence we need to arrest the smuggling gang. But if you are up for a bit of adventure, perhaps..."

Officer Hou provided Ernest with a camera, a phone, and a disguise.

He took a job hauling equipment at the docks and kept his ears open for news of any suspicious activities.

It wasn't long before the gentle rhino was summoned by a concerned co-worker. The worker cautiously led him to an area where some men were unloading crates from a big ship that had just arrived from Africa. Ernest heard lots of strange birdcalls and animal sounds coming from inside the rusty, battered ship.

Chipper-chit-chack! Oo-waaaa-wa–WOK!

The men seemed secretive. They did not want to be seen. Officer Hou had told Ernest to film the smugglers, but to avoid getting too close. Once he got some good footage, he was to phone Officer Hou.

On the bustling waterfront, notorious international wildlife smuggler, Richard Buscot (pronounced *Boo-sco*), unloaded his cargo of elephant ivory, rhino horns, and rare animals. Much of this shipment had come from the wild forests and savannahs of Africa. Baby chimpanzees stared pitifully from behind the boards of cramped crates. Colorful tropical birds, unable to fly away, cried out in despair inside their cold and dirty cages. No one seemed to care at all about the animals and their desperate situation.

A Chinese buyer known as "Silk Jacket," accompanied by his men, met Buscot at the docks.

"Lovely ivory...taken from forest elephants, no?" asked Silk Jacket as he gazed greedily upon the merchandise. "And such fine rhino horns! I will give you $20,000 for those!"

Buscot agreed to the price. "Tonight at Club Shanghai," Silk Jacket announced, "drinks are on me!"

Ernest, hiding in the background, saw the horns and thought about how they had only recently belonged to proud rhinoceroses galloping across golden brown savannahs in Africa. His heart sank as he secretly filmed the smugglers.

Suddenly, Silk Jacket noticed a suspicious figure behind them. Ernest had forgotten what Officer Hou had told him, and had gotten a bit too close.

"Hey, Mister! You can't film us!" Silk Jacket yelled. And then he noticed Ernest's prominent triangular nose. "Hey, he's a rhino! Get him! Cut off his horns, they'll be worth a fortune!"

His men charged toward Ernest, waving their razor-sharp
machetes. Ernest fell back in terror. He had gotten himself
into a fine pickle now!

Fortunately, in the nick of time, Ernest remembered one of the lessons he had learned from his wild cousins.

He lowered his head, snorted out a warning, and then charged the smugglers rhino-style, head down and horn up! The smugglers, caught off guard, found themselves hurled into the air like popcorn by the rampaging rhinoceros.

When Officer Hou and her wildlife protection agents arrived, she found Ernest sitting atop a wiggling pile of unhappy smugglers.

"I've got 'em!" shouted the beaming rhinoceros. "And best of all, I filmed the whole thing."

"Not bad for your first mission!" exclaimed Officer Hou. "Why, you just caught the two most notorious wildlife smugglers in Asia. You're a hero to hundreds of rhinos, elephants, and other wild animals!"

44

At a formal ceremony the following week, Officer Hou pinned a royal panda medal on Ernest's cravat.

"Of course," she told him, "your great achievement is only a first step. Wildlife all over the world is still under terrible threat from poaching. Can we work together in the future?"

"You can count on me," Ernest answered solemnly.

The next day he flew back to England.

46

Ernest was still daydreaming about his action-packed adventure when he arrived at the airport near Puddington. He was happy to be back in England.

That evening, over dinner at his house, Ernest recounted his adventures to a spellbound Sartorius and their old friends, Mr. and Mrs. Hippopoddington.

When he heard about Ernest's courageous charge into the ring of wildlife smugglers, Sartorius' throat rumbled in an elephantine chuckle.

"So you still have some wild rhinoceros in you after all!"

"I suppose I do," Ernest said proudly. "Why don't you and I plan a trip to visit Africa and meet your elephant cousins?"

Later that evening, after the Hippopoddingtons had departed and the softening sun had descended behind the rolling hills, the two friends finished their *rainbow swirlers* and retired inside to begin planning their next adventure.

"My dear Sartorius," chortled Ernest, "perhaps on our trip you'll find there's still a bit of wild elephant in you, too!"

47

RHINOCEROSES:

These are beautiful animals related to horses and tapirs that can be seen galloping across the savannahs of tropical Africa and Asia. Due to his unusual upbringing in England, Ernest Horningway's ancestry is a bit uncertain, but, given his rather pointy upper lip, he is probably a black rhinoceros (Latin name: *Diceros bicornis*). This is the type of wild rhinoceros Ernest visited in Kenya. Also in Africa lives the white rhinoceros (*Ceratotherium simum*), with wider lips. Both African species have two horns over their noses. A one-horned rhinoceros lives in India. The much smaller and hairier rhinos of Sumatra and Java like to wallow in mud pits in swampy forests. All rhinoceros species are gravely endangered because people mistakenly think that their horns are a kind of medicine.

49

ELEPHANTS:

Ernest's wise old friend, Ogoro Sartorius, is an African savannah elephant (*Loxodonta africana*). There is a smaller kind living in Africa as well, the forest elephant (*Loxodonta cyclotis*), and then there is the Asian elephant, which can be distinguished by its smaller ears and females lacking tusks. Elephants used to be found all over the world, and also in the form of mighty mammoths and mastodons, but today, because people kill them for their meat and ivory, they only survive in a few scattered places. Unfortunately, because people think their ivory tusks (which are really just giant "buck teeth" the elephants use to joust with one another, as defensive weapons and for digging up food) are beautiful, they love to carve them into figurines and wear them as jewelry. For this reason, the last remaining elephants are being killed wherever they are found. We must work together as a species to stop the senseless slaughter of these ancient and wise beings.

50

Is the international trade in wild animals and their parts. Hunters, who are called poachers when the hunting is illegal, kill or capture wildlife. Much of this trade is illegal, and it generates billions of dollars in profits each year for poachers and smugglers.

Some examples are:

1. Bushmeat, or wild animals killed for food. This meat can be eaten by local people, or can be shipped to big cities or even flown to other countries to be sold.

2. Babies of mother animals who have been killed for meat can be sold as pets or to zoos, circuses, and biomedical labs.

3. Ivory from the tusks of African and Asian elephants fetches high prices in markets around the world. Ivory has been used to make trinkets, piano keys, billiard balls, and decorative carvings. Currently the biggest market by far is in Asia, but a lot is bought in the United

States as well. Elephants are rapidly being driven to extinction due to this voracious desire for ivory.

4. As Ernest discovered, rhinoceros horn is valued as traditional medicine in Asia (despite being made of the same substance as fingernails, and thus worthless as medicine) and is also used to make traditional dagger handles in the Middle East. Rhinoceroses will soon disappear from the wild if this trade cannot be stopped.

WILDLIFE CONSERVATION:

Refers to efforts made by governments, citizens, and organized groups to preserve the plants and animals of

planet Earth from being destroyed, degraded or consumed. In this book, Ernest worked with Chinese government authorities to arrest people who were illegally selling wild animals and their parts. Many brave wildlife guards around the world patrol national parks and other protected zones trying to stop poachers from killing the animals and selling them for profit.

Rainbow Swirler:

Is a delightful, fruity concoction favored by Ernest. Rainbow swirlers are said to be produced in only one specialty juicer's shop not far from Puddington. It is prepared in layers: Start from the bottom up with stripes of grape, kale and green tea. Then top these treats with layers of pineapple, blue cherry and delicious red raspberry. The mystery is, how are the layers kept separate? Only the juicer knows! The rainbow swirler is best served chilled, accompanied by tasty crumpets and olives.

About the Author

Photo courtesy of
Wojciech Kazanecki

Dr. Cleve Hicks received his Ph.D. from the University of Amsterdam in 2010. He has spent much of the past 15 years living and working in the Congo Basin in Africa, studying the behavior of our close evolutionary cousins, the gorillas and chimpanzees. While exploring some of the most beautiful areas of biodiversity on the planet, he came face to face with enchanting beings such as forest elephants, giant pangolins, African grey parrots, and giant forest hogs. At the same time, he found himself on a collision course with encroaching waves of human "development," in the form of logging companies, mining operations, and bushmeat networks threatening the existence of these magnificent creatures, as well as of traditional human societies.

Today Cleve teaches classes on non-human culture at the Faculty of Artes Liberales of the University of Warsaw, while continuing his research on African apes at the Max Planck Institute of Evolutionary Anthropology in Leipzig, Germany.

He hopes that Ernest's tale will delight and inform children around the world, and inspire the policy-makers of the future to place more consideration on the needs of the embattled wildlife of planet Earth.

Some of the proceeds of the book will go toward putting new boots on the feet of wildlife guards in Africa and providing them with other much-needed supplies. These are the brave men and women who risk their lives daily to protect our planet's natural heritage.

Ernest's message is that we owe more respect to the enchanting animals with whom we share the earth, who deserve to be seen as more than meat on a plate, powdered horn "medicine," or an ivory trinket on a key chain.

The author investigates a chimpanzee ground nest in the Bili-Gangu Forest, DR Congo, with colleagues (l-r) Ligada Faustin, Mbolibie Cyprien, and Ephrem Mpaka, 2012.